THE CURSED

SUPERNATURAL & ENCHANTED POEMS

RENE M GERRITS

Tellwell Talent
www.tellwell.ca

ISBN
978-0-2288-3067-2 (Hardcover)
978-0-2288-3066-5 (Paperback)
978-0-2288-3068-9 (eBook)

*To Karen Gerrits, who, infinite in her patience
to be my listener, reader, and supporter.
Above all these titles, I call her Mother.*

Table of Contents

Dancing Moonlight

Water swiftly runs downstream.
Moonlight dances upon the surface.
Oh, what a spectacle to be seen.
The moonlight running with the stream.

Where it touches is where it gleams,
As it runs with the stream.

Rays of light break through the surface.
Casting shadows on fish defiantly
Running against the stream.

Truth

The body is but a host
Life, is but a passage
Imagination is immortal.

Fantasy

A silent plain of windswept grass.
Where the sun beats down is here it basks.
Light unfurls through the trees.
Through the shifting canopy.

A sky lit red, a blazing fire.
Make crimson hue as it soars higher.
Here, a place of magic, of fantasy.
A place where beauty lies where the eye can see.

Where dragons bask and soar so high.
They matt the grass and light the sky.
A phoenix sun, a mystical moon.
Bring creatures life and creatures doom.

Mountains that scale the landscape so high.
Their tops turn white as they touch the sky.
Down below; forests and meadows carved with lakes.

This here for me is the place to be.
In my mind, in fantasy.
A place of bliss and tranquillity.

In this place of fantasy.
In all the tranquillity.
There is one that dwarfs all beauty.
You.

Northern Lights

A poetic phenomena exploding in the sky.
A pulsating matrix, seems as though it
Were alive.

Its colours so vibrant, harmonious and true.
The luminescent lights, so beautiful all threw.
For, if ever I could create such wonder.
I would do so, just for you.

Moonlit Embrace

The stars, they shine a distant hue.
The moon; an eerie light.
Shadows dance across your face.
Oh such beauty to behold
On this pale night.

Gazing at your silhouette; so fair against
The moonlit horizon.
Wondering deep into your eyes, that capture
The awe from the starlit sky.

Hair that flows like a tranquil stream.
A smile that's oh so warm.
Here with you, I'd love to be.
In your arms for eternity.

But one bliss filled embrace is all I need
To feel an eternity.
On this pale night.

Serenity in the Mind

A meadow broad.
A babbling stream.
Mountainous landscapes jutting
Frosty teeth.
Lays a land of blissful peace.

A gentle breeze sways among tall trees.
A golden sun and peaceful moon.
Stars wink high in the radiant night sky.

This the place to be, a world of
Complete serenity.
But such a gallant existence can
Only thrive in the realm that is.
My mind.

Nomad

What heavens yield and Hell burns over,
Where demons cannot conjure.
I walk abroad this earthly plain
In search of what is yonder.

Loves Temple

Love is like a temple.
Created on a solid foundation with the belief
That the structural and emotional integrity
Will withstand all forces hurled upon it.
Some prove false and submit to the crumbling decay
Of time or persistent abuse.
Others are pure and endure all that
Comes to clash upon its formidable walls.

Love is like a temple.
It must be pampered and maintained.
For trials and tribulations attempt to
Rock its very foundations.
Cracks that are caused by errors which may
Separate two pieces of stone. May tear two
Lovers apart. Leaving in its
Wake, a tattered relationship.
A strong enough love, knows no loss.

Sunlight Shattered Figure

Sunlight shatters the morning canopy,
Radiant light brings to life the silent dew
Creeping on the forest floor.
Trees creak and howl in the morning wind as it
Comes to life in the new day.

A gallant form moves below the canopy,
Silently gliding from tree to tree.

A shaggy cloak and oversize hood extend
An eerie presence upon the figure.

Leaves kick up as he glides on by,
Only to be captured by the breeze.

So grand a life he would have led
If he had not embarked on this quest instead.

Looming Doom

She sits in waiting.
Darkness looming.
Strangers drawing nigh.

Fog is creeping.
Trees are creaking.
Armour is clanking dulcet.

She leaps from hiding.
Through with spying.
A hunger for heroes' blood.

Teeth are gleaming.
Talons seeming,
Sharp as his own sword

A knight hath fallen.
The swamp has caught him.
And slowly sinks from sight.

On The Wicker Bridge

On an evening roaming,
I came to a wicker bridge.
There sat an aged man,
Upon its wicker ledge.

He winked at me and smiled,
Stretching his leather face.
So I promptly sat beside him
And stared into his space.

An old dirt road I had not seen
Before, stretching beyond
The rolling hills.
Bound by the river I sat above.
And I'm perched there still.

I asked him why he sat there.
As a curious young inquisitor.
He said he was not sure but was
Sure to see a reminder.

I asked him where he came from
To sit on this rigid bridge.
He said that memory failed him,
But was somewhere over yonder ridge.
I said that I too was lost, and could
Not find my way back home.
I asked if he would be my friend,
And together we would roam.

At that the old man looked at me,
With sorrow in his eyes.

He said I must find my own way home,
And venture without him.

He made a promise years ago,
With that his thoughts grew dim.
"I feel for you my new young friend
And hope what you seek you find.
For unlike me; a long life it had been,
You've died before your time."

The Story Teller

There once was an old chap who was always perched
upon his porch.
Sitting in his rocking chair, smoking his sweet tobacco pipe.
Peeling with an old weathered knife.
Fruit that was not quite ripe.

Every day he'd stop me as by I strode.
And ask me to sit at the steps on the porch of his abode.
His pipe smoke would linger in the still warm air,
As I humoured him in the stories that he told.
Of great adventures he would rant,
On the seas in nature's wrath.
In tall ancient forests or in nights darkest black.
"Oh what a grand tale to tell."
He'd always boast he had,
So for me to sit down next to him I could see made him
glad.

But now he does not sit there.
The chair does rock on its own.
The wind weepily howls as the lonesome deck does moan.
Now once a year I come back home and perch upon that
porch.
And tell the stories of that old man to those who would
lend an ear.

I tell tales of my own exploring.
Of when I was weak and bold, to those who would listen,
To the young man grown old.
For I know that soon it will be my time.
I feel death perched by my side.
In the hopes of sparking one's young mind.
So the stories don't go cold.

The Bell Toll Thrice

The bell doth toll a first ring droll
A persistent echo of the second bell ring
That seems to sing the song of death as it sets
Its ring for the bell toll thrice making shadows
Shudder to pay the price for the ghosts of souls
Unforgiven for deeds unforgotten.
To weigh heavy on the living as they pass
By day to suffer at night is where they must
Stay in the darkness,
The dreary abode down the
Brimstone road they strode.
A suffering pain cannot be shut
Out for even in death they feel its bout
It rings again, its song is long and ominous,
The torture of their memory stabs from the
Shadow to pierce their sorrow.
It runs like oil and spills on the road,
Vaporous in the air with screams of despair.
All to be heard by those under the bell.

Eternal Embrace

Hearts pressed tight.
Bosoms heaving
Holding you in lustful arms,
Hard in believing,
To behold such beauty without going blind.

Nay shall it fade,
Nor shall it diminish.
The ravages of time,
You will ever evade.

As I age, I weep for your youth,
You still hold me tight,
With soft velvet hands.

Until time overcomes me,
Taking me away to eternal sleep.
You lay me down,
Within your heart.

Whispers on the Tide

I stand among the rolling plains,
As the wind blows, it whispers your name.
Thoughts of you drift through my mind.
Feelings for you, I carry in my heart.

The trees; they sway to and fro,
Against the wind as it blows.
I whisper you're name against the wind.
Against its tide that never ends.

The forest sings its hollowed song,
Against the waves that crash along.
A shoreline that stretches
To where our eyes can see.

Where the maw of the ocean swallows
Your whispers for me.

The Ghost Ship

Feel the chill of midnight's quill
Fog rolls in through the air stands still.
The waters stir, subtle at first, a churning heard in the
distance.
The lighthouse beacon fades from sight.
Shrouded by the fog of the night.
The flapping of sails, catching a breeze
The whistle of wind between old wood beams
The fog horn blows, a warning for those
Still on the water forebode
The reef grows and come to life
Jutting from waters where once out of sight.
Rotting timbers and the scent of gun powder
Linger in the still night air.
There, to be seen off the shore
The spectre of a ship that once was but no more.
Water churns, all around it is cull.
Mist seeps from holes in the hull.
Tattered sails flap as if caught in a breeze
The ship does moan from forces unseen.
Torn ropes and loose rigging hang in despair
Give a sense of the sorrow clinging to the air.
Upon the deck, a ghostly crew
Tirelessly labour their last duties as if nothing's askew.
Their moans echo their sorrow
The fog retreats as the ship passes by
Taking with it, the sailor's cries.
Their moans turn to sobs as though saying goodbye
True rest for them is far from nigh.

Forever Friends

Tracks are silent, cold and still.
Nothing to be heard but owl's eerie call.
The trees, like statues, do not move.
Their shadows cast by light of moon.
Clouds linger in the sky.
Casting their features as they roll by.
Midnight dew trickles down.
Icy steel laid to ground.
Glittering in the midnight light.
Shining back, the stars, their light.
Footfalls heard in the night.
Disturb the silence but not the light.
Whispers heard in the air as the footfalls
Make their way up the track.
Whispers turn to laughter and glee as they make
Their way merrily.
Each forgetting to look back
Nor hearing the train on the track.
That sorrowful day, as they strode home.
The train had come, to them unknown.
For two best friends, it was too late.
That very train held their fate.
The train no longer travels down,
The tracks, grown in and nowhere bound.
But the laughter of two best friends,
Their conversation never ends.
Their voices echo on the breeze.
Through the midnight statue trees.
Down forgotten tracks, they strode along.
Their last moments rehearsed on and on.
Passed the crosses that bear their names.
They fade into the morning haze.

Sea of Sorrow

Sorrow strikes
It takes you away
Leaving only, feelings of dismay

Sadness blurs the reality around you
Yearning binds it's tendrils about you

The idea of hope and the will to fight
Are as blind as the darkest pitch of night.

Swiftly be the sorrow that strikes
Leaving you blind in the darkest of nights
In a sea of sadness.

The Gargoyle

Sitting atop its stone perch.
The austere beast gawks abroad the world.
Powerless to negotiate from the bleak bitter setting.
Unable to conceive nor ponder freedom.

Star Lit

Stars burn in the night,
Casting spears of soft light.
Illuminate, so fair,
Your silhouette in the midnight air.
To glisten on your flowing hair,
Past your shoulders like a gentle stream.
Such a wild light, untamed, so true.
Harnessed only by your eyes.
Casting back through beautiful contrast.
So mysterious, so daring.
So frightened and not caring.
Bosoms lift with each breath.
In the light they are caressed.
So enchanting in the light,
As you stand before my sight.
And as the sun breaks the sky.
It's burning light reaching high.
Casting off your silhouette,
Romance of night now shed.
Revealing to me, Opulent Beauty.
No longer concealed by soft kissing shadows.
Now touched by morning hue.
The truest of beauty I have ever beheld.
You.

In a Dream

Last night I dreamed of you and me
In a world of ecstasy
Within a haze, in a shroud
A forested grove all around
Arm in arm, embraced to be
One in One, you and me.
As mist pulls back your flowing hair
Your eyes gaze up, your skin so fair
Our arms are bound about our backs
Our fingers run so gently.
To hear you speak into my ear
Your melodious voice so calming
This is where I yearn to be
In your arms in ecstasy
To caress your hair like warm silken sheets
Running through my fingers
Your luscious lips I beg to kiss
To steel but only one
Oh, what a sight it is for me
To behold such opulent beauty
To embrace what true love gives
To be in love, to be in bliss
To be in love with another soul
Like my own, to make us whole
I dare not let go
As I wake in the shroud of night
To feel you close beside me
I wrap my arms and pull you close
And close my eyes to kiss you again

The Hound

In the darkness oppressed and forlorn
Stalks the hound so frightfully dreary

Eyes are glowing in the gloom
A torrent of death
An omen of doom

Patiently watching passer-by
Picking and choosing who will die.

With a snarl, howl, growl and a cry
The last to be heard
For the miss-fortunate passer-by.

The Riverboat

Down the river the old man must row
Rowing his oar to and fro
Down the river he does not make haste
Ferrying the souls to Hade's gate

Cursed to never loose his grip
Drop the oar nor let it slip

Oh what a fate, to suffer this way
To ferry souls till the end of days
He begs, pleads and wishes most
But Death cannot come to the river boat.

I Vow

Love is a quest not taken alone
In your arms, together we roam.
This path of life, the trails we choose,
The trials we take, the fights we lose.
Hand in hand, eternal embrace, our hearts are
stronger
Than time and fate.
My love for you is pure and strong
To you I vow to Cherish each day,
To love only you in our special way
To always be true,
Devout faithfulness only to you.
This is my vow, to love and to hold,
With only you, I promise to grow old.
I offer my shoulders to catch your tears,
To rest your head and quell your fears.
I promise to listen to whatever you say.
To watch you grow more beautiful
With each passing day.
My lips for you, can only smile,
They yearn to kiss yours all the while.
My arms are yours to keep you close, to hold you tight,
To never let go.
I want to wake up with you as the sun rises high
I want to bed you as the moon takes the sky
I offer my hands as a symbol of strength
They will always protect you.
I give you my legs for stability and flight
I offer my chest,
This houses my heart.
I promise to you forever
This is my promise, my vow to you.

The heart in my chest beats only for you.
And so, as we venture forth sharing moments in life.
Will you do me the honour,
Of taking my heart and
Becoming my wife.

A Heavy Note

Air; placid, hot and still
Stones jut from the hardened earth.
Every step a heavy note
Down rows of stone he strode.

Standing still in the cold kissing air.
Eerie solemn of the night licking the tips of his standing
hairs.
A grotesque note in the silent dead.
The names of those no longer read.
Monuments pose in memorial.

Time has ravaged and eaten away
Those not remembered but forever stay.
Fatigue set in and stones have downed.
Consumed by dirt; forever drowned
By grasses that glow in daunting night.
Basking in moons eerie light.
Shadows cast and reach aloft.
Drowning out the souls of lost.

Every stone he passes by.
A beckoning call or a frightening cry.
Through the cold moonlight cast.
He fails to see her, he's searching vast.
His seasoned eyes lost and sore
Gaze beyond death's vague door.

Every step a heavy note
As he walks a path of stone.
A silhouette ne'er to be seen.
His love, his loss somewhere between.
He comes upon a weathered gate.

A seasoned fence.
Turning back; he searches again.
To find his love, unbeknownst to him.
She is still alive.

Flowers bloom and start to fade.
With each passing of the days.
Perched beside his own gravestone.
He waits for her to come home.

Kiss of the Gorgon

Through the dark and murky gloom.
He failed to see his pending doom.
In the still air of the night.
A gleaming blade in dancing light.
Swallowed up in the abyss.
Lady in wait; a deadly kiss.

A tight embrace so warm and wet.
The luscious kiss of regret.
If only he had been more aware.
Of the Gorgon and her lair.
Her eyes tell tale of lost and lone.
The last he sees as he turns to stone.

Lovers Fate

She waits in meadow in the eve
Signs of her lover ne'er to be seen.

A general caught wind of his daughter's plans.
A soldier has paid for his defection.
His horse; does flee without its master.

His sword and musket lay in a ditch.
Stained with blood that was his last.
Her name he calls; his final cry.
Swallowed by the forest as he dies.

The trees; they grow in gnarled form.
They resound his cries from years before.
Branches weep, a saddened gloom.
O'er hanging her solitary tomb.

The hollow shell that stood in wait.
Only to share her lover's fate.

Disembodied

A voice; it echoes through the house.
Disembodied in dismay.
It lowly moans and slowly bays.

Stomping up and down the stairs.
Rapping walls and throwing chairs.

Crying out to those who dwell.
In the house where he fell.

Death had touched him in mid-life.
As he lay beside his wife.

Many years has since passed by.
His wife moved out and long since died.

Grieved and stricken he calls and cries.
Her name resounds before living eyes.

Unaware she waits for him.
In another place, another time.

Three Bells

The first bell doth chime, its chorus; divine.
I met your gaze on the first bell ring,
Drawn to it, the song it sings.
And so it began on the first bell chime.

The second doth announce its melodious tone,
It's in this melody we make our first home.
And as this song wavers, it begins to slow.
Comes the chorus of wedding bells;
A new chapter to sow.

In this song, the longest it is,
Came all of our children with a ding and a chime.
This carries the second bell's song for the rest of
It's time.

We grow, we play, we evolve you see,
Making our way to proverbial bell three.
As this bell makes its song known.
A long, soft whispering chime.
I lay you down one final time.

As you rest eternally, to the heavens I will plea.
I want to say "I love you" a hundred more times.
Oh how I yearn for my bell to chime.

Epic poem

Here I sit and ponder, and much to my dismay.
My love I wish to confess, though, I cannot find a way.

Roses are too mundane.
Chocolates are overdone.
Cards are of poor character.
Dinner would be a dine and run.

I'm truly at a loss, as I watch you from afar.
I would like to lavish you with jewellery.
I'd even buy a car!

A ring would be ideal;
To place on your finger blessed.
But one from a gum machine,
I'd surly be laid to rest.

How can I express my true love for you?
To make my presence known.
How can I show you my devotion?

It will have to be this poem…

The Church

I revisited the church, my marriage;
That deed was done.
Pews and chancel decorated and
Glinting religious decorum;
From the ceiling hung.

I could see the people,
Dressed in ceremonial best.
Proclaiming their well wishes;
Our marriage to be blessed.

But from the darkness came that thing.
From the gloom, ever peering.
Through my soul, ever searing.
From the darkness loomed the beast.
From the darkness this creature's gaze
Ne'er ceased.

It likes to whisper from the darkness to the light.
From the ramblings it takes delight, ever
Rambling on my hardship, my strife.
"T'was I." It reposes.
"T'was I; who took your wife."

O'er the years, our battle waged.
Now those years have fallen to past,
And I am nearing the end of my days.

To the church, I have come.
To the church to see it done.
In the darkness that is looming.
From the darkness, ever brooding.

Came the whispers of the creature.
From under pews and behind features.
T'is here; I wage the battle of life.
T'is here, I reunite with my wife.

A Tortured Poet

Spurred by darkness, things unknowing.
My craft in life hath become my blight.
A forlorn room; I sit and write.
Write a prose of eerie night.
Write a piece that will stir and fright.
In the darkness ever looming.
With my quill, words of brooding.
On the pages ever turning,
Fingers bleeding, ever hurting.

Words of lost loves and those once adored.
Tales of darkness, of light that's fading.
Prose of those in pain creating, words I once adored.
But in the darkness I aphore.
In the calming of the night.
In the pitch; the words, they write.
Though, I've lost sight of the word; adore.

The quill; it moves of will and mind.
Writing words that are not mine.
Dipped in blood that is my pain.
I dare not stop, I try in vain.
Spirits of the darkness have me.
Through my skill they tortuously craft me.
Bent to a will that is not mine.
Taken by something not evil nor divine.

Crafting words that lay cold.
Ne'er heard and ne'er told.
Locked away for evermore,
In brooding darkness I aphore.

Writing the thoughts of the dead,
Ne'er to be heard, only read.
In life I was a poet adored, in death I am a vector.
In brooding darkness I aphore.

The Nightmare

Grim; is the tale of that thing,
Above my door it perches.
With eyes brooding, ever swooning
All corners of the room.

Always glaring, ne'er fairing
A chance to look away.
For in my room; it's gaze so cold
Here; it's cursed to stay.

Nay to waver, nor to falter.
Its austere position, it dare not alter.
Hovering, looking,
Ever looking, ne'er to produce a sound.

Tiny talons clutch the wood,
Poised to move as if it could.
Yearning to move as though it should.

Perched alone, the beast.
This tiny thing.
Glaring, glaring. Ever staring.
Piercing my very soul.

Its eyes; unkindly, as though surmising
What fate whilst befall me.
By window pane, I gaze and strain.
Under covers; I hide my shame.

The moon; it lingers in the sky.
Piercing me with ghostly eye.
Reaching out with rays like fingers,
Caressing my quivering features.

Its light, it stretches across the room.
A ghostly luminescence.
Ghastly fingers of the moon.
Kissing that thing, that horrid thing.
Perched, glaring.
An omen of doom.
Mated in the brooding night.
They glare, they stare.
They stir and fright.

In the midst of my pain.
Whimpering, wailing. Silently wailing.
This moon mated thing is my bane.
For every night the moon doth show,
The nightmare cometh.
Into my soul, fear is sows.

This haunting, grisly mated beast.
It ne'er stops nor whilst not cease.
Through its terrible gaze it stakes.
A claim upon my soul it stakes.
It sits and waits, my soul to take.

Bonnie Dundee

There is a lass with eyes set solely for me.
Those are the eyes of Miss. Bonnie Dundee.

She's beautiful and proud and so full of glee.
Infectious is the laughter of Miss. Bonnie Dundee.

Her song; like a siren, draws men from the sea.
The melodious voice of Miss. Bonnie Dundee.

By her side I'll forever be.
I take up my bride.
Mrs. Bonnie Dundee.

The Castle

A testament to time, a window to past.
A monument to sieges.
Scars on its walls where missiles had been cast.
After years in the hundreds
It still stands fast.

The Muse

The Muse; she takes delight.
Guiding my hand by lamplight.
Whispering stories into my mind.
Conducting my pen, instructing the rhyme.

My imagination; she brings to bloom.
Stories of love, creatures of doom.
I feel her presence, sense her perfume.
From her sweet soft whisperings posy.

Pro's entrancing and poems enchanting.
Through me, what conjuring's I so adore.
For via my craft.
The Muse's words out-pour.

Fantastical

Through slits in helm, he sets upon.
His quarries sword has been drawn.
Through loom of night and light of day.
Blades clash, but to their dismay.
To neither one had fallen prey.

But from the distant mountain bays.
A fearsome dragon, on knights it preys.
At my station; with my pen.
The fearless knights, the dragon rends.
In their boldness, in their blunder.
The dragon did cast asunder.

Embedded and entranced.
The pen; in its rhythmic dance.
To life before me.
Forges my world of fantasy.

The Forbidden Love of Jenna Rose Keating

A tragic romance destined first meeting.
Sorrowful tale of two souls pleading,
Loves misguided needle weaving.
The forbidden love of Jenna Rose Keating.

Our bond in knowing was forbidden,
In our vigilance, kept it hidden.
Though we knew time was fleeting,
Our secret place of solace retreating.
The forbidden love of Jenna Rose Keating.

Torn apart by worlds conceiving,
Conspiring, deceiving.
A final farewell, our hearts were bleeding.
I shall Nevermore, dis-remember meeting
The Beautiful, Jenna Rose Keating.

The Highwayman

In his carriage, an evening late.
On route home, a man of state.
Night's befalling, a sense of dread.
A ghostly moon sails overhead,
Its looming light beckons the dead.

When to the carriage, came a dreadful blow.
The hanging lantern swayed to and fro,
Casting shadows in its glow.

Betrayed by the light, he could tell.
A foreboding figure on the carriage dwell.
Horses galloped with all their might,
Grievously fleeing from the blight.
Their pace; frantic, full of fright.

From the door; pushed ajar.
Daring a glance, peering out,
Risk a chance.
Through misty gloom, air that's wet.
A figure upon the carriage beset.

Upon the carriage in the coachman's stead,
A spectre of a highwayman, a skeletal head.
It glowed an eerie, ominous hue.
A cold light that equalled the moon.

With a hand; grotesquely withered,
He beckoned for him to come hither.
His face was bone and paper skin,
His eyes were wild, his lips were thin.
With a horrid voice he spoke.
A ghastly, gruesome churning croak.

"On this; an annual charade,
For this night a debt must be paid.
If you decline what is to be named,
Away with your soul, for it will be claimed."

At this the man shuddered, stammered and stuttered.
"Name your price." With a quiver he muttered.
The highwayman smiled a ghoulish grin
Through bared teeth and paper thin skin.

From his coat with gloomy hands,
The highwayman brandished golden strands.
On the spectre's request the man did know,
He could tell from the bow.
A lock of hair was to be his strife.
For the highwayman's price was his wife.

"You ghostly, ghastly thing so dreary,
I must pose to you this query.
What thing or beast might you be?
Tell me please, make me see.
Spirit or creature of the dark abyss,
Before I answer you must honour me this."

The highwayman laughed, then he sighed,
Turning his gaze to the sky.
"The moon has faces, one you see.
Two of them, you think there be.
I am face number three."

"For the damned and debts I deem owed,
I claim all souls who ride my roads.
Your time is near, it comes soon
For you've been marked by the moon.
Its light has touched you in its wane,
So I've been sent, your soul to claim."

"But if you pay the debt marked by the second face,
Another soul will take your place.

Beware; the price you pay to live is steep.
For it will be your wife we reap."

With quivering hand, he took the hair, held it tight.
Knowing this would be his last night.
"If it's my wife to go with you, I tell you highwayman.
I cannot pay this debt due."

Time had passed without him showing.
The wife; widowed, without her knowing.
Then one night in her despair,
Upon her door was a lock of hair.
Held by a pin from her husband's coat.
To the door, a written note.
I will always love you to the moon,
And shall return to see you soon.
For keep an eye on the clearest nights
And look for my coming in the moons waning light.

The Caller

He came from faraway said he to she,
A place not close to here.

"Oh why have you called to my doorstep dear sir?
Why have you sought me out?"

"Your humming my dear,
Your melodious sweet tune,
Could lift a heart of its drought.
Oh come with me sweet lass,
Sail from these domestic shores."

"To Where? She bayed, slightly afraid.
Would I venture across the sea?
Once we're set upon your land,
Would at your side I'd be?"

"Come with me across the Sea
To where you will forever be
Adorned with lavish comforts
Befitting royalty.
He brandished an heirloom from his coat,
A crest of royalty.
Adorned with gold and fine jewels,
None before she'd seen."

A certain joy welled up within,
Her heart was a flutter with glee.
She left her home and all she owned
To sail across the sea.

Upon the ship, she did board.
Humming merrily.
It had only been six leagues they travelled
She noticed his false humanity.

Beneath the shroud of this mortal suitor
Was a creature of the night.
The devil smiled a grin so vile,
For in this he took delight.
I will take you from your home,
Relieve you of your life.
Henceforth dear lass,
You will be my wife.

She begged and pleaded,
She yearned to go home
But his guffaws only grew higher.
And in an instant, they were gone.
The sea had turned to fire.

Rest in Peace

In my bed, near to dead,
A figure stands before my head.

I cannot see who it may be,
Yet she softly speaks to me
Words of tranquility.

As my eyes begin to close
She gently hum's and kisses my nose.

Overcome by peace where I lie,
My soul relaxes and I die.

The Thing

As I lay down to sleep,
Under covers, I dare not peek.
From the closet comes a creak.
A ghastly thing; dreary and bleak.
Teeth and talons caress my sheets,
Where I hide, frightened and meek.
I wish this night would turn to day
So this thing would go away.

The Wish

The coffee was warm,
Conversation; deep.
Forgetting myself in your
Opal eyes.
Not a clashing of intellects
But a merging of the minds.
What power you have,
I cannot resist.

Your red lips are so perfect
As they traverse your words.
Oh, how they catch the light.
Your hair, how it flows as a
Waterfall tumbles so fine,
Your collarbone; so fair.

I envy your fingers as they
Toy with your necklace,
So gently caressing your neck.

Oh, your smile; so gorgeous.
Your cheekbones are hoarders
As they catch it up and keep
It for themselves.

Your chest does heave,
As you laugh with glee and
You reach out to take a hand.
But my heart; it does break
For it is not my hand you take.

Reality is cruel and harsh,
It is not me you want
I am the one with the pot.
A well of pity for me and
Resentment for he;
The one that you so desire.

I am just a young man,
That is all that I am
To the years you have over me.
Oh how I wish you could see
There is so much more to me
Than the server at a coffee shop.

Peggy Bloor The Black Dog Witch of Black Bog Moor

Beware traveller of the black moor blight.
Travel by day, never by night.
Beware, the sign says of Peggy Bloor.
The one who dwells in Black Bog Moor.

Be wary of the hound, ever by her side,
A beast so large that the witch can ride.
Twelve lengths of men in its stride.

Beware the hound's howl, the witch's scowl.
For if you encounter these stated, you must know
You have been slated.
For on your path they will remain,
And will become your life's bane.

Stay to the road,
Never follow the Black Bog's light.
For you will surely be led astray,
In the moor you will forever stay.
Once claimed, you will be
The Black Dog Witch's property.

To risk safe passage through the moor,
Pay a tithe upon her door.
Smear your blood into the grain.
Announce your payment in blood and pain.
If she accepts, you will remain.
Dare she deem you false,
Your blood she will drain.

Beware the hound that stalks at night.
If in the dark you must travel,
Mask your scent and keep from sight.
Else it will hunt you like a blight
Until you sate its appetite.
Make for the peaks beyond the eastern ridge.
There you will cross the eastern bridge.
If you make it before the black dog bays,
You may live the rest of your days.
But if you falter, stammer or stray,
You may be rendered the black dog's prey.

To quell the hound, keep it at bay,
Open a jar, locket or spray
The tears of the dead, away it will stay.

Cross the bridge over the river twitch.
If you look back, surly you will see the witch.
Keep ahead if you value your eyes,
For if you look back, they will be her prize.

If you make it across before the hound bays,
Looking ahead and not led astray,
You will hear a cackle and the witch say.
They know your face and in waiting will stay,
For you have to come back the very same way.

The Ghost

A ghost does hover before my door,
Merely feet above the floor.
The apparition does taunt me in this way,
In my house, night and day.

As if waiting for some person or thing.
The door to open or the bell to ring.
Dressed in garments; Victorian's best
A gaping wound in her chest.

A gown that nearly touches the floor.
Soaked and dripping;
A puddle of blood before the door.

I cannot help feel pity and excited
For this poor soul who had been smited.
What an act of jealousy,
Betrayal or treachery.

Before the door she is content to stay,
Hovering in this way.
Every night and every day.
Watching the door, never stray.

Oh, the people she keeps away.
That flee from the door or
Refuse to stay.

A complexion of despair,
Green eyes so fair.
Beautiful locks that hang
In her hair.

Each day and every night.
I look upon her and I lament
And wish her time had not been spent.

I wish she was more like me
Of flesh and blood, then she would see.
I've fallen in love.

The Sirens

They sleep upon the island reefs.
To all the sailors; a chorus of grief.
Their voices carried by the wind and rain,
To all the vessels; a captain's bane.
For the souls of ships and crew they claim,
To the loved ones awaiting at the shore; their pain.

But for the sirens who sing to gain
The crew that fall to their lament,
The ships upon the reefs now broken and bent
The hulls splintered, their sails spent.
For the loved ones who stand before the shore who cry
Begging to be held, yet saying goodbye.

For those who make it home do pine,
Ever entranced by the sirens rhyme.
To the sea they yearn to be
To answer the sirens beckoning plea.
Until their days of living are spent.
They will forever hear the sirens lament.

The Bane of the Knight who had fallen to Shame

He walks with a limp and a weathered cane,
His honor; shattered and his valor; slain.
A body withered by age and strain.
The bane of the knight who had fallen to shame.

His sword is pitted, the edges are dull.
His armor hangs with patches of rust,
The shine has long left and has lost its lust.
His sigil on his armor faintly remains,
The bane of the knight who had fallen to shame.

His banner; torn and draped to the floor,
A banner called to service no more.
Stained with the victories of his foes slain.
The bane of the knight who had fallen to shame.

The world was now blind to his pain,
No more enemies, beasts nor lands to reclaim.
If only he had a squire to train,
Mayhaps there are books that tell stories of his name.
Through tales regaled he would ever remain.
The bane of the knight who had fallen to shame.

Then one day, he went away.
At his abode he dare not stay,
To die in bed where he lay.
Dawned his armour and his sword,
His banner became his cloak.
The day the knight conquered his bane,
He knew he would never return home again.
One final quest in search of his fame.
The quest of the knight who is rising from shame.

The Visit

Late one night whilst I was dreaming,
Into my chambers came a woman weeping.
Before my bed, sobbing, creeping.

To behold her in her whimsical ghostly gore,
This thing that hovers before my door.
I shuddered; stricken, filled with horror
As the spirit moved from my door.
Not one part of it touched the floor,
This floating spectre of ghastly gore.

She beckoned me as if to follow,
Calling my name in a voice that's hollow.
Resounding off the walls
Now seeming tall and foreboding.
Engulfed in darkness looming
With a spirit brooding.
This spirit in its whimsical
Ghostly, ghastly gore.
Beckoning to me before my door.

I mustered courage before this thing.
"What omen are you? On this night bring.
Or to my mind; a conjuring?
What news from the grave do you bring?
Why present to me your suffering?
Such a grotesque spectral thing,
A torturous lament you sing."

But her cries merely grew louder,
The air; colder.
And my position did grow bolder.
My anger festered as a fire smoulders
At this ghostly, ghastly thing of gore.

Launching myself from my bed,
Toward this thing; defiantly I tread.
This spectral grisly thing of gore,
To watch it fade and cry no more.

Three more nights in this way,
In my abode, this ghost did stay.
Amidst mournful cries, my name
She bayed.
To the moon and heavens I prayed.
What forces beset her upon me?
A will to let me sleep no more.
This ghostly, ghastly thing of gore.

Then one night as I imbibed;
Indulging a bitter by fireside.
As the moon reclaimed the sky,
There was no spirit, lament nor cry.

Glass to bottle, a generous pour.
A victorious toast and then one more.
This ghostly, ghastly thing of gore
Hath gone from my abode for evermore.
To thrice imbibe, I did stutter,
For the bottle made me shudder.
On this bottle was my bane,
For the label bore a name.
A name; to mine so similar,
A name; to mine was almost the same.

"Hath this conjuring come to my life to save?
Mayahaps an omen of doom?
Or of death to proclaim?"
T'was no matter.
Events came to fruition, I could see.
If only I had known her message was so dire.
For in that drink, I expired.

The Crypt stand cold and stone

Cold and stone, forgotten by time.
Remnant of a past; its people left behind.
What secrets are held within its keep,
Of what people and deeds, it dare not speak.

Left in time, it stands alone.
Only seen by those who roam.
Frosted windows forbid a peek,
Of secrets through years,
Those daring to seek.

It only relinquishes a written name,
Of those inside to rest are lain.
For those who the crypt brandishes their name,
Have long since gone.

The Misgiven

There is one misgiven child,
Who; unlike his brothers,
Had grown to be wild.

Out to the world, he yearned to see,
Away from all people he wanted to be.
Where his adventures would take him,
He never knew.
With each destination, his imagination grew.

After many years, one could surmise,
The boy; now a man, had grown wise.
Until one day, in a distant village,
He did find. A beautiful girl,
Her smile was kind.

A man so strapping and debonair
Who equaled her beauty and
Obsidian hair.
They held their hearts for a very long time.
He settled in her village and became
One of their kind.

In time there came a beckon call,
From the mountains, heard by all.
His wife was summoned to come home,
With their children; she would leave him alone.
With a kiss on his lips and a sign of farewell,
She returned to the heavens from where she fell.
An aging man; still debonair,
Embraced by the beast of despair.

He climbed to the highest peaks.
His wife and children, he did seek.
The love for his wife he could never quell,
And refused to accept his family's farewell.

People do talk, stories were told,
Of how the man; devoted and bold.
They always said he was one of a kind
And mayhaps one day, his family will find.

The Knight and the Hydra

A knight so brave came to the cave
Where the hydra preys on people and ships
All nights and days.

With many heads, eyes of dread.
Peering from the darkness
Over corpses its fallen dead.

The gallant knight; he hurled a spear
And watching the darkness, it disappear.
Striking the hydra.
From that moment hence,
The battle commence.

Waging by the seaside, the hydra;
With its venomous spray,
Filled the air where the knight met his prey.
Pitting his armor and killing his steed,
Collapsing in one final "nay."
A singular head reached over the dead
Grasping the horse to drag it away.
With a flash of his sword
The knight severed the head and
There it will forever stay.
Eight more heads and titanic legs
Came clawing from the depths of the cave,
To face the knight on the cliffs
Where the sea waves sprayed.

A shield in one hand, a sword in the other,
The knight stood defiantly against the
Venomous jaws and razor sharp claws
Wearing at his shield.

Then in a moment of skill and luck,
The knight; his sword, he did wield
Striking the beast in the chest
Where its black heart is concealed.

But in its death throws it hurled the knight
On to the rocks with only his shield.
A gout of venom in a turbulent spray
Covered the knight amidst sea waves spray,
Parts of his armor fell away.

Locked in combat they will forever stay,
On the rocks by the seaside spray.
On the cliffs overlooking the oceans turbulent tide.
The knight and the hydra, together died.

Dance of the Sparrow

A sparrow perches on a
Gnarled branch, swaying in the breeze.
Dancing in the gusty currents,
Its tiny talons seized.
A rhythmic dance of bird and branch
Until one departs the other.

In the Morning

Spring peepers cry.
Morning birds sing their song.
Perched on a log, a lizard plays its lute.
Branches quake as the squirrels wake
Darting tree to tree.
Morning light in beams and rays

Break through the morning canopy.
Other beasts, from dens do peak
As they stir from their sleep
And get on with the day.
For every morning amidst the forest
Begin this very way.

Borne Away.

I mourn, wish, yearn and hope
With us you were here to stay.
But alas; time and fate have
Borne your breath away.

Through day and night
A modicum of delight;
Your memory is here to stay.
Yet the pain of loss tears at
My heart for your
Breath had been borne away.

Solace in knowing, the pain is gone
And in time I too will move on.
For one last embrace I would gladly pay,
To the heavens I will loudly bay.
In my solace, quietly pine.
For your breath had been
Borne away.

Now a new chapter in my life must start.
I will forever keep you in my heart,
Cherish your love, day to day.
For when I hold my hand to my chest,
I know, your breath is there to stay.

Though your guidance is quiet
And seemingly far away.
I close my eyes and hear your voice.
Your breath is here to stay.

Should the night cause me to shudder,
Yearning for light of day.
I recall your swooning touch,
Your breath is here to stay.

Until my time is over,
Until my end of days.
I will always carry you with me.
Your breath is here to stay.

My Michelle

I love you so very much
Missing you hurts my heart.
Soon we will be in one another's
Embrace, and for a time
Ne'er have to depart.

Your love is as a candle that burns
Chasing away the night.
Yet as all things that flicker in elegance,
To I; a guiding light.

To hold someone so deeply
So close to the heart is pain.
Yet embrace the hurt, so far apart,
T'is there you'll ever remain.

I wish to say I love you,
A thousand times and more.
For you are my one and only,
My girl I so adore.

I love you to the moon and back
To miss your sweet embrace.
For where the light casts on your bed
I wish to take its place.

For you, my beautiful Michelle.
My girl I so adore.
With every beating of our hearts
I love you more and more.

To my falling star,
My rose in fields.
My beginning and my end.
I love you so very much.
…..Ren….

The Vampire Bride.

Clouds like tall ships sail high,
Blotting the moon as they pass by.
From the crypts a figure creeps,
Into the abode he doth sneak.

An invitation from hence before,
He passes the threshold that
Is the door.
Into the bedchamber he
Silently skulks.
Over a damsel, stricken and gaunt.

Though her skin was pale,
One could see.
She was the picture of innocence,
Of pure beauty.

He ran his fingers down her cheek,
In adoration, so elegant and meek.
She opened her eyes,
Tired and sunk.
For under his charm,
She was entirely drunk.

She placed her cheek into his palm,
Beautifully placid, she kept her calm.
With a heavy sigh,
She gazed deeply into his eyes.
She did not stammer, shout nor cry.
They twinkled like the brightest
Star in the night sky.
He smelt of autumn and
Sweet cherry pie.

He had luscious flowing ebony hair,
Every girl's fancy of a dashing debonair.
He smiled sweetly and whispered "Hello."
Revealing fangs,
In the moonlight did glow.

"Oh my love, I have returned at last,
On this night your bonds to mortality
Shall finally pass.
Sail with me to emerald shores,
My castle awaits,
What is mine is now yours.
Come with me at the peak of the tide,
Depart with me and be my bride."

Her cheeks; they flushed with
A kind of glee.
But there was fear in her eyes,
He could see.
"Will it hurt?" She quivered.
"Will I feel pain? And my
Family my love, will I see them again?"

"No and yes."
He softly uttered, then gave her a kiss
That sent her a flutter.
With a final bite,
Her body fell numb, and
To the vampire, she did succumb.

On the tallest ship they sailed away,
And reached the emerald shores
On the eleventh day.
There they remained side by side.
A debonair vampire and his
Beautiful bride.

The Folly

Along came a knight
On a stallion bold.
Passing a tower,
Weathered and old.

Peering over the turret,
A damsel fair,
She had rosy cheeks and
Long golden hair.

"Hark! Sir Knight
On such a gallant beast,
I can tell by your banner
You come from the East."

He turned his gaze up to
The maiden fair.
He was struck by her beauty
And long golden hair.

"Hark! Young maiden
Of beauty so fair.
I am charged to slay a beast
When I discover its lair."

"A beast you say?"
Mused the lady fair.
"Does it live in the water?
The land? Or the air?
Does it live in the trees?
Or the mountain peaks?
Does is come out at night?
Is it malicious? Or meek?"

"I don't know my lady,
Enchantress so fair.
My beautiful damsel with
Long golden hair."

"Maybe I am the beast."
She boldly stated.
"And this is my guise
You've underestimated."

"You are no beast!"
He laughed aloud.
"For if you are the beast
Then relinquish your shroud.
You are a beautiful damsel
On high, for if you were a beast,
Surly you would die."

She chuckled so sweetly,
This girl on high.
She disarmed the knight
With an adoring *Sigh.*
This beautiful, enchanting
Damsel so fair.
With a melodious voice
And long golden hair.

"That armour looks heavy,
You so well adorn.
Why not come in to rest
And depart in the morn."

The knight was delighted to
Accept her request, He
Dismounted his steed and
Sent it to rest.
One night of comfort and

He shall resume his quest.
Inside he met the damsel so fair,
With radiant eyes and
Long golden hair.

Seven years passed since
He entered the tower.
The knight emerged
Withered and sour.
Drained of his youth,
The knight cried in despair.
For in his arrogance and folly,
He entered the beasts lair.

The Soldier

Bombs exploding,
Lighting the night sky.
The soldier gazed at his
Comrade; wounded
Who had tears in his eyes.

He wished and begged for the soldier
Not to let him die, and
Together they held tight as
Bullets whizzed by.

Under the cover of a battle
Torn night.
The silhouettes of two soldiers
Could be seen chancing their flight.

Through barbed wire and fox holes,
With every laboured breath,
The land was barren.
It was rank with death.

Every passing moment,
A growing sense of dread.
As the soldier carried his comrade
Over the fallen dead.

The soldier soon knew
That his friend did die,
For as they reminisced of home
There came no reply.

Knowing that his comrade
Had passed away,

He continued to carry him for
A night and a day.

Holding his friend fast,
The soldier did *sigh.*
For now he was alone,
And started to cry.

He came upon a meadow
With a pond and tall trees.
Flowers and grasses that
Swayed in the breeze.

The soldier took a knee,
Propping his comrade
Against a tree.
Before the pond, facing the sky,
The soldier bid his friend
One final goodbye.

Sitting by his comrade,
He would fight no more.
For he had found this place
Not ravaged by war.

Unbuttoning his coat,
He could only see red.
Struck by a bullet, the
Night they had fled.

Leaning on his friend,
His life had been spent.
The soldier closed his eyes
For he was content.

The Cursed

He glared out the window,
A grievous expression
Laced his face.

For there was something lurking
At a lumbering pace.
"What is this lumbering creature
That stricken me with fear.
This horrid lumbering creature,
What ill fate brings it here."

He rushed to the second story
And threw open the shutters hard.
There was this loathsome looking
Creature, lumbering through the yard.

A threadbare cloak draped over its body,
A tattered hood covered its head.
And when it trained its eyes upon him,
His heart welled up with dread.

He ran to the banister and
Watched it push open the door.
He became stricken with terror
As it let its cloak fall to the floor.

It sniffed the air and rumbled,
A low and ominous growl.
It looked up at him, bared its teeth
And greeted him with a scowl.

It stood upright like a man.
It had the body of a Grimm.

Its hair was black and shaggy,
Its ears were long and thin.

"What are you."
Mustered the man, in a voice
That cracked and quivered.
The notion of acknowledging it
Made the stricken man shiver.
Its eyes were wide and sunken,
Like glowing amber gems.
Its maw and teeth were malicious,
Death was all over them.

It then bowed and gestured
As though it invaded his abode
In good faith.
Then spoke in an unnatural voice,
The man listened as it spake.

"I am the bane of this estate
You inherited some time ago.
Now on this night of waxing moon
In you; the seeds of curse I shall sow.
For I am your father's father,
And the fathers before him.
Many generations ago, on this night
We were cursed by the Grimm.
The past you need not know,
For this families legacy to ensure.
Then you, my blood extension
This curse you must endure."

The man drew a pistol and
Trained it on the thing.
"I do not bid you entry into this
Vessel, I do not accept what you bring.
Be gone from my abode you horrid thing.
Though shalt not pollute my soul
With such a foul offering."

The beast merely grinned
Now at the top of the stairs.
The man was caught up in its eyes,
That amber, ominous glare.

"You think you have power,
Your life cannot be saved.
When you accepted this estate,
Your choices had been waved."

The room was filled with the pistols roar
And the beast was hurled to the floor.
But it chuckled and stated as it rose.

"What threat to me do you think you pose?
For I am your curse, your very bane.
By your hand I cannot be slain.
Shoot me, stab me, fight or flee.
Wherever you go I will always be.
On the day you choose to submit
I shall be there, the curse to inflict."

"I tell you beast of ill tiding,
There is no such curse my family
Is hiding.
Depart from my abode,
Back to where you came.
Be gone from my presence for
I am burdened with no such shame."

"You claim to me you bear no shame,
Yet my very presence is your family to blame."

It stood before him, this massive beast,
With obsidian claws and deathly teeth.

"Where had your father gone?
And the fathers before him?
They were hunted and taken by

This curse; the curse of the Grimm.
Long have I waited to what forces
Did I plea. Long have a hunted,
Waited to see.
Now with your arrival,
From the bonds of the curse, I am free."

"You have humanity in you sir beast,
For you were human before.
So it is your humanity I do implore.
Spare this life sir beast, let the curse
Die with thee.
I beg you on the blood we share,
Set this family free.
For you are my father's father and the
Many fathers before.
Save this family from this curse,
This I do implore."

The beast looked upon him with
Eyes of sad and sympathy.
Then hoisted the man into the air.

"I commend you on your effort,
Yet what you fail to see.
You; my distant blood relation,
Are the only one who can set me free.
This curse cannot be broken,
Merely passed through family.
If I am to rid myself of this
Torturous life, then cursed
You must be."

The beast bore down upon him,
Attacking savagely.
The man cried out in protest,
Wailing in agony.
It laid its curse upon its kin

And from its bonds would soon
Be free.

The man awoke on the floor,
In his own blood and gore.
Not a mark nor a scar did his
Body bore.
The beast stood over him,
Its cloak it did adorn.

"From you sir I take my leave,
I shall depart in the morn.
I am so sorry my distant blood
For inflicting such a sorrow.
But now you see, I am free
And I shan't be the same on the
Morrow.
On the next moon of waxing,
The curse will be at its height.
On that night of waxing,
You will feel the curse's blight."

"Damn you beast,
You wretched thing, this ancient
Family curse you bring.
I am the last of my bloodline,
I have no other kin.
I should not have to pay for
Your eternal sin."

He heard the beast say as it
Walked out the door.
"Then you are the beast for evermore."

Deceived

Late one night whilst he was reading
A book quite ancient, the literature seeming
To conjure forlorn images in his mind.

Sipping a brandy, he did explore
Several chapters then some more,
Casting stories on the floor
Before his very eyes.

Invested, intrigued, he could not stop,
This fantastical book he dare not drop.
All these stories he did explore,
Brought to life upon the floor
Until the chapters were no more.

Upon the bookshelf he did replace,
Then to his chair he did retrace
To sip his brandy in a quiet space
Save the spits and spatters of the
Fireplace.

When in the chair beside him,
Sat a hooded figure with no face,
Merely blackness in its place.
It smelt of musty books and
Ancient oak and he
Welled up with dread as
It turned and spoke.

"I am neither living nor dead
For I am the spirit of the book you read.
The pages you turned,
The stories told go back to times

Forgotten and old.
One hundred years since
Our pages have turned.
And for a story, the book does yearn,
Before the clock chimes twelve
Tomorrow night, a story for
The book you must write."

The man sat beguiling this foreboding
Spectre whilst drawing long sips
From his auburn nectar.

"And what if I fail to write for thee?
What if by the midnight stroke
I possess no story?"

"From you the book will
Draw its due, Through yourself
It will see it through.
Part of the book you will be
A faceless page such as me.
Three hundred of us and one more;
Faceless wraiths for evermore.
Bound by this book we too had read,
On our very beings it had fed.
Our bodies themselves have
Strengthened its bind,
Helping it withstand the
Ravages of time.
This book on your shelf
Is a beast in itself.
For it was not created by
woman nor man but archaic forces
With a sinister hands.
So write I say!
Grab parchment and pen
And at Twelve O Clock chime
You will see me then."

The man; he wrote to save his life.
He wrote stories of joy
And stories of strife.

He wrote stories of heroes
Setting loved ones free.
Stories of sailors who were
Damned by the sea.
He wrote of great loves and their bane,
He wrote of knights and castles
And great dragons slain.

The man; he wrote so vigorously,
He dared not to falter, he failed to see.
His face was fading,
A wraith he would be.

By the midnight chime,
The man was not there.
Only the book was in his chair

So, if you happen across a book;
Its stories it does tell.
Close it quick, that curiosity
Dare not quell.
For if you do give it a look
You will become one with the book.

Entombed

Dark is the hour the clock doth chime,
Foreboding in that stroke,
The witching time.

Shadows crawl,
From corners creep.
From depths of darkness
The dead do peep.

Voices moan from wall to wall
In this hour, the dead do call.
Hands like talons reach and grasp,
Her troubled soul they try to clasp.

The house does seem to be alive,
As restless dead call and writhe.
Stricken with fright she calls and screams,
From her abode she tries to flee.

Window pains; like evil eyes strain,
Through their malice rays of moonlight stream,
she am trapped in a nightmarish dream.
For corridors stretch and wind,
Twisting and warping her tortured mind.

Suffer the wrath of creatures only she can see,
In this hour beset upon me,
Tearing through this house in her lament.

When rays of sun welcome a new day
she can exit the heavy oak threshold
and run away.

But the house will beckon and
she must head its call.
For she is entombed in the wall,
Above the fireplace that watches the door.
There she will stay for evermore.

Lay you Low

Late one evening whilst he was digging,
shovelling, heaving.
A six foot pit,
A coffin keeping.

The last of the sun faded, sleeping.
The evening dew,
From the ground, creeping.
Gravestones; silently standing, weeping.

On the coffin of smallish size
Sits a girl, two coins for eyes.
Amidst her woes, wails and cries.
"Why?" She pleads.
"Did I die?"

"This my dear, I do not know.
I dig the holes and put you low.
I cannot tell you how or why."
To the girl was his reply.

"Why so deep must I go?
In this place of wood and woe"

"T'is the way."
He did say.
"So you cannot climb out and walk away.
People are foolish and full of dread,
They fear the notion of walking dead.
You cannot climb out, this makes it so,
And to the heavens you will go."

"I hear my parents my mother does cry."

"That is what mom's do when daughters die."

"I cannot cry, not a tear, I sense their
emotions yet I do not fear."

"I am laying you down for your eternal sleep,
You are dead so you cannot weep.
In the coffin you must go,
Close the lid so I can lay you low."

He laid her down and said goodbye,
She did not object, query nor cry.

"You will be okay."
He said with a *sigh.*
"I was the same when I did die."

Lightning Source UK Ltd.
Milton Keynes UK
UKHW040703211020
371973UK00002B/252